YOU / ME = Ann Perkins
YOU / ME = Leslie Knope

(CIRCLE THE ANSWERS)

YOU TAUGHT ME THAT
TRUE FRIENDSHIP
MEANS

_____.

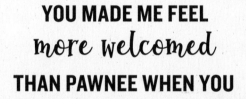

YOU MADE ME FEEL *more welcomed* THAN PAWNEE WHEN YOU

_____.

REMEMBER
THAT TIME WE
_____?

I'D BE LOST WITHOUT YOUR

_____.

OUR FRIENDSHIP
MAKES ME FEEL

_____.

I love how you

_____.

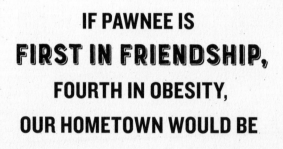

IF PAWNEE IS **FIRST IN FRIENDSHIP,** FOURTH IN OBESITY, OUR HOMETOWN WOULD BE _____.

I KNEW YOU WERE MY
FOREVER GALENTINE
WHEN

_____.

YOU WERE A
POETIC AND NOBLE
LAND-MERMAID
WHEN YOU

_____.

Your biggest strengths

ARE _____

AND _____.

I BELIEVE IN YOU **MORE**
THAN LESLIE BELIEVES IN

_____.

IF WE DID A KARAOKE DUET,

OUR SONG WOULD BE

_____.

YOU MAKE ME **LAUGH**
THE HARDEST WHEN YOU

_____.

You love

**MORE THAN LESLIE LOVES WAFFLES
AND POLITICAL PURSUITS.**

YOU WERE THE
EPITOME OF A BEAUTIFUL
RULE-BREAKING MOTH
WHEN YOU

_____.

YOU DISLIKE

**MORE THAN ANN REGRETTED
WATCHING ALL EIGHT
HARRY POTTER MOVIES.**

YOU WOULD MAKE A
GOOD PRESIDENT
BECAUSE

_____.

IF WE WORE

matching hats,

THEY WOULD SAY

_____

AND

_____ .

THE **BEST PRANK** YOU
EVER PLAYED WAS WHEN

_____.

I KNOW I CAN ALWAYS COUNT ON YOU TO

_____.

I WOULD

IF WE COULDN'T BE
FRIENDS ANYMORE.

OUR
friendship pact
SAYS

_____.

MY FAVORITE
NICKNAME
FOR YOU IS

_____.

WE'VE BEEN MISTAKEN
FOR A COUPLE AT LEAST

_____

TIMES NOW.

YOU REMIND ME
OF **ANN** WHEN YOU

_____

AND **LESLIE** WHEN YOU

_____ .

FARWELL LI'L SEBASTIAN

WE'LL MISS YOU

_____

IS LIKE OUR OWN
Li'l Sebastian.

YOU PROVED JUST HOW

LOYAL YOU ARE WHEN YOU

_____.

IF YOU RAN FOR OFFICE,

YOUR CAMPAIGN SLOGAN

WOULD SAY

_____.

OUR **SIGNATURE**
DANCE MOVE IS

_____.

**THE BEST WAY WE
CELEBRATE THE SPIRIT OF**
Galentine's Day **IS BY**

_____.

THE THING WE HAVE
MOST IN **COMMON** IS

_____.

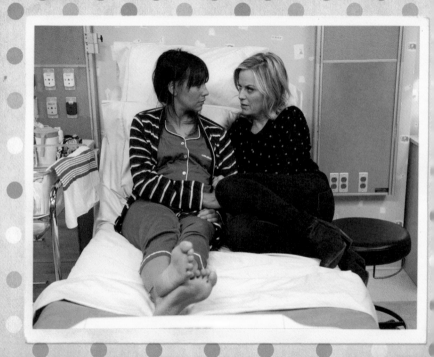

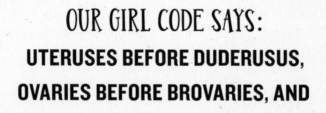

OUR GIRL CODE SAYS:
UTERUSES BEFORE DUDERUSUS,
OVARIES BEFORE BROVARIES, AND
_____.

YOU'RE **MORE** THAN
A FRIEND, YOU'RE MY
_____.

YOU ALWAYS
treat yo' self
TO

_____.

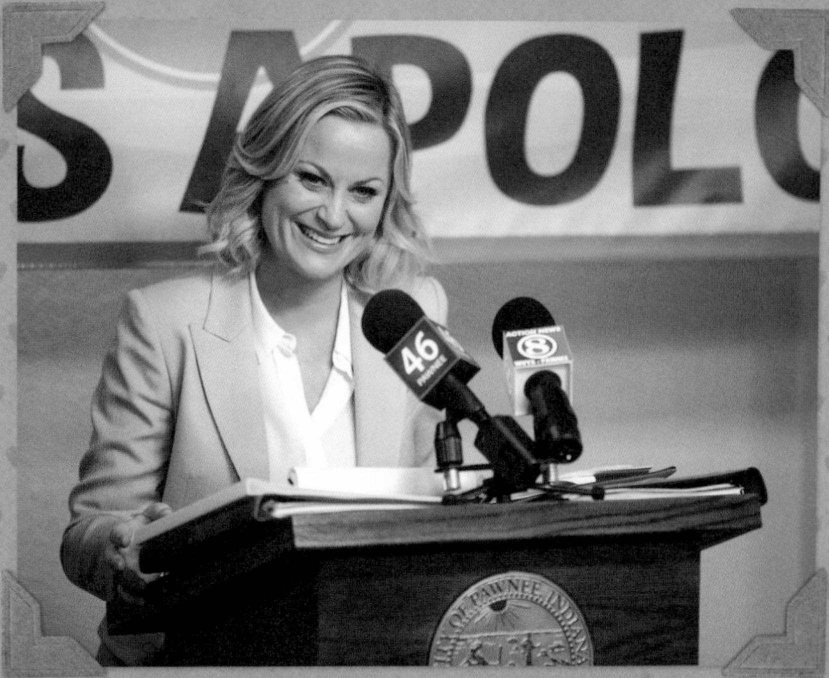
46
PAWNEE
ACTION NEWS
8

LESLIE'S CELEBRITY CRUSH IS JOE BIDEN; YOURS IS

_____.

YOUR ADVICE ABOUT

_____

COULD RIVAL RON SWANSON'S QUIET WISDOM.

THAT TIME WE

———————————

WAS  **WORSE** THAN WHEN LESLIE AND ANN GOT DRUNK ON SHOTS OF SNAKE JUICE.

YOU TALENTED, BRILLIANT,

rainbow-infused

_____.

IF YOU HAD TO **CHOOSE**
BETWEEN BEN WYATT, ANDY DWYER,
AND RON SWANSON, YOU'D CHOOSE
_____.

YOU THINK

_____

IS DUMBER **THAN CALZONES.**

THE MOST **MEANINGFUL**
GIFT YOU'VE EVER GIVEN ME IS

_____.

WE BOTH AGREE THAT

the most important

THINGS IN LIFE ARE

FRIENDS, WAFFLES, AND

_____.

IF **ANYONE** WERE TO
EVER HURT YOU I WOULD

_____.

THE TITLE OF OUR
FRIENDSHIP SCRAPBOOK
WOULD BE

_____.

I LOVE YOU
MORE THAN

_____.

You perfect sunflower.

RP Studio™
Hachette Book Group
1290 Avenue of the Americas, New York, NY 10104
www.runningpress.com
@Running_Press

Printed in China

First Edition: May 2020

Published by RP Studio, an imprint of Perseus Books, LLC, a subsidiary of Hachette
Book Group, Inc. The RP Studio name and logo is a trademark of the Hachette Book Group.

The publisher is not responsible for websites (or their content) that are not owned by the publisher.

Text by Christine Kopaczewski.
Design by Marissa Raybuck.

ISBN: 978-0-7624-9840-6

1010

10 9 8 7 6 5 4 3 2 1